The Mysterious Growing Moon

by Chris K. Powell

illustrated by Kenneth Vincent

Harcourt
SCHOOL PUBLISHERS

Copyright © by Harcourt, Inc.

All rights reserved. No part of this publication may be reproduced or transmitted in any form or by any means, electronic or mechanical, including photocopy, recording, or any information storage and retrieval system, without permission in writing from the publisher.

Requests for permission to make copies of any part of the work should be addressed to School Permissions and Copyrights, Harcourt, Inc., 6277 Sea Harbor Drive, Orlando, Florida 32887-6777. Fax: 407-345-2418.

HARCOURT and the Harcourt Logo are trademarks of Harcourt, Inc., registered in the United States of America and/or other jurisdictions.

Printed in China

ISBN 10: 0-15-351529-5
ISBN 13: 978-0-15-351529-3

Ordering Options
ISBN 10: 0-15-351214-8 (Grade 4 Advanced Collection)
ISBN 13: 978-0-15-351214-8 (Grade 4 Advanced Collection)
ISBN 10: 0-15-358119-0 (package of 5)
ISBN 13: 978-0-15-358119-9 (package of 5)

If you have received these materials as examination copies free of charge, Harcourt School Publishers retains title to the materials and they may not be resold. Resale of examination copies is strictly prohibited and is illegal.

Possession of this publication in print format does not entitle users to convert this publication, or any portion of it, into electronic format.

1 2 3 4 5 6 7 8 9 10 985 12 11 10 09 08 07 06

Nick Moskal was ten years old. He lived with his mother and father, and his sister, Sasha. They had a wide backyard with several large trees and a simple garden that Nick's mother worked on every spring. Nick and his sister walked or rode their bikes to school every day.

Nick's father was a computer expert who helped design the computer system at the company where he worked. Sometimes when the neighbors had problems with their computers, they would ask Mr. Moskal to have a look. He always did so because he liked his neighbors and was happy to help them out. Nick's mother worked part time at a flower shop in town.

One day, in the middle of summer, Nick was digging a hole in his backyard. He wanted to create a small "lake" for his toy soldiers to cross during a battle.

While digging the hole, Nick noticed an odd looking stone in the ground. He dug it up with his shovel, took a closer look at it, and saw that the stone was a peculiar shade of white. It wasn't a milky white like some other rocks he had seen before, but bright white—almost shining.

Nick went to his room and placed the rock on his windowsill. He had a feeling there was something special about it.

The next morning, Nick woke to a drab, rainy day. He glanced out his window at the gray, overcast sky, and then he noticed that strange rock from yesterday on his windowsill. "Now, just what kind of rock are you?" he thought.

After eating breakfast, Nick pulled out some encyclopedias from the bookshelves and looked up *rock* and *stone*. He studied the photographs of many different rocks, looking for one that matched his bright white one. He compared the rocks in the pictures to his. Marble was a light colored rock, but his was much shinier and brighter. Quartz looked similar, but it, too, was a little bit duller than his rock. An hour passed, and after looking at all the photographs and reading the descriptions, Nick was still unable to identify his rock.

He set the rock back on the windowsill and played around on the computer. Then Nick went to his friend Harry's house.

As the hours passed that day, the sky slowly began to clear. By the time the Moskals ate dinner at seven o'clock, the sun had finally come out from behind the clouds. Nick and Sasha went out front and threw a football around, but as the sun went down and the moon came up, they headed back inside. On the way, Nick glanced up at the moon. Something seemed different to him.

"Hey, Sasha, look at the moon," Nick said.

"What about it—it's the moon," replied Sasha.

"Don't you think it looks a little larger than normal?" Nick asked.

Just then, their father came out and took a look. "Sometimes the moon looks big, sometimes it looks small," he explained. "You see, when the moon is up in the sky, you don't see any other object next to it. There's nothing to compare it to. When you see it low in the sky, though, like tonight, you can see it next to other objects, like trees. Compared to the trees, the moon looks really huge."

Nick loved how his father could always explain things. Nick looked back at the moon. It seemed to be about twice as wide as the top of the maple tree.

Nick became very interested in the moon. He looked it up in the encyclopedia and learned about the moon's different phases: full moon, half moon, crescent moon, and so on.

What his father had said about the size of the moon especially fascinated Nick, so the next evening, he went to the backyard and observed the moon at the same time as the night before. He compared its size to the top of the maple tree. What Nick saw, though, concerned him: the moon was clearly larger than it had been the night before. "Maybe I measured it wrong last night," Nick said to himself. "Could I have been that far off?"

Just then Nick heard voices. He looked to his right into the neighbor's backyard. Mrs. Wilkins and her daughter Elizabeth were out there, pointing to the moon. Nick ran right over and asked excitedly, "It looks bigger, doesn't it?"

"Definitely," replied Mrs. Wilkins. "I've never seen the moon look like this in my entire life."

Nick felt a tingle of fear rise up his spine as he ran into the house and found his father reading in the living room. "Dad, the moon looks even bigger than last night, and I know I did my measurements right because I compared it to the maple tree," Nick exclaimed.

"Easy now, slow down. Let's just go take a look," said his father calmly. Nick felt relieved that his dad would now explain exactly what was happening. His dad could figure anything out—from computer problems to the growing moon.

When they went to the backyard and looked up, though, Nick saw a look of confusion come across his father's face. Mr. Moskal's eyebrows scrunched close together. "Why that's strange, it certainly does look larger," he said.

"What's happening?" Nick said, trembling.

The next night, Nick dashed out to the backyard
at sunset, waiting to observe the moon. It glowed
brightly, like a huge spotlight, and dominated the
sky. It was both beautiful and frightening. "I really
don't understand, Dad," Nick said.

"I'm afraid I don't either, Nick," Dad said. "I've
done some reading about light and objects, and
I thought it was an optical illusion, which would
mean the moon only *looked* larger. I can see,
though, that it's no illusion."

Each evening, the moon grew larger, and before
long the whole town noticed it. People expressed
fears that something awful was going to happen,
like the moon would get too large and bump into
the earth. Others said that maybe the moon wasn't
getting larger but just moving closer to the earth.

In time, people across the nation became aware of the situation. Each day, there were special reports on TV. Experts were asked what they thought was happening and why, but none of them had any answers. All Nick knew was that each night, the moon took up a larger and larger portion of the sky.

Most nights, people in Nick's neighborhood stood on the sidewalks in front of their homes and looked at the moon. Since the moon was so much larger, they could see fascinating details, like craters and plains, that had never been visible before.

One night in early August, a full month after the whole moon episode began, one of Nick's family's neighbors, Mr. Stevens, appeared on the street. The neighbors, who had gathered outside to look at the moon, thought this odd as Mr. Stevens was a hermit who only occasionally ventured from his house. Though rather strange, he was a timid, kind man.

As he walked down the street, Mr. Stevens looked up at the moon and repeated, "Little and bright, big and bright, all the same." The neighbors looked at him, confused by his strange words, and then Mr. Stevens disappeared back into his house. Those words, though, stuck in Nick's head: *little and bright, big and bright.* The moon was obviously *big* and bright now, but what was *little* and bright?

With this thought on his mind, Nick went up to his bedroom to lie down. Before going to bed, he walked to the window to look at the moon again. It was huge and seemed to cover almost all of the sky. In front of Nick, on the windowsill, was the odd white rock. He studied it—that odd white rock, that *little and bright* white rock. "That's it!" Nick exclaimed.

He instantly grabbed the rock, rushed to the backyard, and returned it to the hole where he had found it. "Be gone now, odd white rock!" Nick said, shoveling the last bits of dirt into the hole.

The next day, Nick paced about the house nervously, waiting for sunset to come. Finally, after dinner, the sun started to go down, and Nick and Harry went to the backyard. They waited for the last bits of light to fade and the moon to appear.

Nick wondered, "Will it be larger?"

"It should appear any moment now," said Harry. Everyone had become a moon expert during the whole ordeal.

Finally, at 8:08 P.M., the moon appeared—and it was its normal size. "Hurrah!" Nick yelled happily. Behind him on the sidewalks, he heard neighbors whooping and cheering, thrilled that the moon—and life—was back to normal.

Nick thought of the strange white rock. Then, just as quickly, he put it out of his mind—forever.

Think Critically

1. What seemed to cause the moon to grow larger?

2. How would you describe Nick?

3. How did people respond to the growing moon?

4. What word means almost the same thing as *dashed* does on page 10?

5. How did this story make you feel?

 Language Arts

Write a Conversation Write a conversation that you and a friend might have had during the events of this story. Later, read your conversation aloud with a partner.

School-Home Connection Share this story with a family member. To make the story more interesting, act out some of the parts.

Word Count: 1,479